Lily Finds a Friend

There was something furry lying under one of the bushes. It was almost hidden under all the leaves, but Lily had spotted it.

"What's that?" Lily woofed to herself.

She dropped down onto her tummy, and crawled towards the furry thing. Gently, she reached out a paw to touch it . . .

All of Jenny Dale's PUPPY TALES books can
be ordered at your local bookshop or are
available by post from Bookpost
(tel: 01624 677237)

Lily Finds a Friend

by Jenny Dale

Illustrated by Susan Hellard

A Working Partners Book

MACMILLAN CHILDREN'S BOOKS

To Yas – who is full of good ideas

Special thanks to Narinder Dhami

First published 2001 by Macmillan Children's Books
a division of Macmillan Publishers Limited
20 New Wharf Road, London N1 9RR
Basingstoke and Oxford
www.panmacmillan.com

Associated companies throughout the world

Created by Working Partners Limited
London W6 0QT

ISBN 0 330 48426 5

57986

A CIP catalogue record for this book is available from
the British Library.

Typeset by SX Composing DTP, Rayleigh, Essex
Printed and bound in Great Britain by Mackays of Chatham plc, Kent

Chapter One

"I'm bored!" Lily woofed crossly.
She slumped down at the top of
the stairs. "Bored, bored, bored!"

Jack, Lily's owner, had gone to
school, and Mrs Harper, Jack's
mum, was at work. Mr Harper
was at home today, but he was
busy putting up a shelf in the

living-room. He'd been sawing and hammering all morning, and he'd shooed Lily out of the room and shut the door. He'd said that Lily was getting under his feet.

"What a cheek!" Lily yapped. She put her nose between her paws and stared gloomily down the stairs. "I was only trying to help. It wasn't *my* fault that Mr Harper dropped the hammer on his toe."

The brown-and-white puppy looked around for something to do. Then she spotted her little rubber ball lying on Jack's bedroom floor. "Oh, great!" Lily yapped, cheering up a bit. "I can play my favourite game."

Lily trotted into Jack's bedroom to get the ball and carried it to the top of the stairs in her mouth. Then she let it go.

THUD! THUD! THUD! The ball bounced loudly down the stairs, with Lily racing after it. She caught it at the bottom, and then dashed back up the stairs again.

THUD! THUD! THUD! Lily

ran down the stairs after the ball again, just as Mr Harper flung the living-room door open.

"Lily!" he called crossly. "Stop making all that noise!"

"Huh!" Lily sniffed. "I'm not the one making all the noise – you are."

Mr Harper went back into the living-room, but this time he left the door open. Lily immediately trotted after him.

She saw that Jack's dad had put up the shelf, and was stacking lots of books on it. Lily wagged her tail. Maybe Mr Harper would play with her now he'd finished his work.

But suddenly there was a loud, cracking noise. The shelf tilted, and one end of it came right off the wall. All the books slid off and landed with a crash on the floor.

"Oh no!" Jack's dad groaned.

"Never mind, Mr Harper," Lily woofed, rubbing her head on his shin. "But you'd better get it fixed, or you're going to be in big trouble with Mrs Harper when she gets home."

Lily left Jack's dad picking up the books, and trotted into the kitchen. There was no way Mr Harper was going to have time to play with her now!

She decided to go outside, to see if her doggy friend Charlie was at home. Charlie lived next door with Sally and her family. Sally was Jack's friend.

Lily nosed her way through her dog flap and bounded out into the garden. "Charlie!" she barked loudly. "Come and play with me. I'm bored." Then she pricked up her ears, waiting for Charlie's answering bark from the other side of the fence.

There was no reply. Charlie must have gone out with Sally's mum, Lily thought gloomily. None of her friends were at home today. Lily seemed to be the only one with nothing to do.

Suddenly Lily had an idea. Her brown eyes lit up. "I could find a *new* friend," she woofed, her tail wagging like crazy. "*Then* I'll have someone to play with."

Lily was so excited by her idea

that she ran round in circles for a bit, trying to catch her tail. Then she sat down, panting, and looked around the garden. Where should she start?

She knew that Jack had asked his mum and dad to make sure there was no way Lily could escape from the garden. The puppy had got lost a few times before and Jack was very worried that it might happen again.

"I promise I won't get lost *this* time, though, Jack!" Lily woofed softly as she sniffed her way along the fence, hoping to find a hole she could squeeze through.

But Jack's mum and dad had made sure there were no gaps in the fence at all. Not even a small one. There was simply no way out.

Lily sat down on the grass, her ears drooping. "I need someone to play with," she whimpered sadly.

Suddenly, she spotted something moving under a big bush right at the bottom of the garden. She jumped up, her sturdy little body quivering. Then she dashed over to investigate.

It was a small, green creature with big, bulging eyes. It hopped out in front of her, and gave a loud CROAK.

"Hello!" Lily panted excitedly. "Will you be my friend?" And she rushed forward to give the creature a big, wet lick.

The creature backed away in
alarm. It croaked even louder
then hopped quickly out of sight.

Lily dived into the bushes after
it. She hadn't explored the bottom
of the garden much because it
was very overgrown. It was so
damp and dark, Lily had always
felt a bit scared. But now she was

determined to find her new friend again.

What was that, half hidden behind that big bush? Lily forgot her chase. She could see a hole in the fence at the bottom of the garden!

Chapter Two

Lily could hardly believe her luck.
First of all, though, she had to
squeeze behind the bush to get a
proper look at the hole.

It wasn't easy. The bush was
very big and bushy indeed. Lily
puffed and panted, her little pink
tongue hanging out, before she

managed to fight her way through.

Feeling excited, Lily peered through the hole, her tail wagging madly. She was looking into a huge, overgrown garden. It was much bigger than hers, with tall trees surrounding it on every side and a lawn in the middle. At the far end of the garden stood a big, old house.

"Hurrah!" Lily barked happily. "This looks brilliant. I hope the people who live here like dogs. I might find a new friend."

Lily began to climb eagerly through the hole. She was halfway through, when suddenly she stopped. Jack's voice had just popped into her head. *"Don't*

*wander off and get lost AGAIN,
Lily,*" he was saying anxiously.

Lily's tail stopped wagging
while she thought about this. "But
I'm not going to get lost, am I?"
she woofed to herself. "I'm only
going to be on the other side of
this hole. I can find my way back
into our garden any time I like."

Her tail started wagging again, and she carried on scrambling through the hole. It was a bit of a struggle to get her chubby little bottom through, but Lily managed it. Then she trotted out onto the lawn and gazed around. The garden seemed even bigger now that she was actually in it.

Lily set off towards the house, her black nose to the ground. There were so many exciting new smells to investigate that she kept veering off into the flower borders and under the bushes. She could smell the scents of people, as well as lots of different animals.

Suddenly, a squirrel darted out of a thick patch of undergrowth and ran across the lawn.

Lily's eyes lit up. "Hello," she woofed, dashing after it. "Be my friend!"

But the squirrel didn't seem very friendly at all. It raced up the trunk of the nearest tree and disappeared among the leaves.

A moment or two later, Lily had to jump out of the way when a conker crashed to the ground very close to her. "How rude!" she yapped, disappointed. "Never mind, I'm sure the people who live here will be a lot nicer." And she bounded across the grass towards the house.

There were some steps leading up to a patio, and beyond it were some glass doors into the house.

Lily panted with excitement as she trotted up the steps and dashed over to the windows. Tail wagging madly, she peered hopefully inside.

An old man was sitting in an armchair in the large living-room, watching TV. He had a tray on his lap with a cup of tea, and a big slice of fruitcake.

Lily licked her lips. She was feeling a bit peckish. "Hello!" she woofed, tapping on the glass with her paw. "I'm Lily, and I *love* cake. Will you be my friend?"

The old man didn't look round. He was too busy watching TV, and he couldn't hear Lily because the sound was turned up so high.

"HELLO-O-OO!" Lily howled

more loudly. "PLEASE BE MY FRIEND!"

But the man still didn't take any notice. Lily felt very disappointed.

"Maybe there's another way into the house," Lily thought determinedly. She had to get inside before all that lovely cake disappeared.

Lily trotted round to the passage at the side of the house. There was another door, but it was firmly shut, and no one came to open it when Lily scratched at it. There was also a tall gate at the end of the passage. Lily guessed it led round to the front of the house. She could hear the cars going up and down the street, although she couldn't see them.

Suddenly, Lily's sturdy little body stiffened. She raised her head and sniffed the air, and her tail began to wag happily. It was a smell and a voice that she'd know anywhere!

"Mum, can Sally come round to play with me tonight?"

It was Jack! He and his mum

and Sally were walking up the street on the other side of the tall gate, on their way home from school.

Lily was just about to bark a loud greeting when she stopped herself. Oh dear, Jack wouldn't be very pleased if he found her in this strange garden, would he? He didn't like her wandering off on her own.

"I'd better get myself back into our garden – and fast!" Lily yapped anxiously. "I just hope I can make it before Jack gets home."

Lily was about to hurtle back towards the hole when she noticed something very strange indeed.

Chapter Three

There was something furry lying under one of the bushes. It was almost hidden under all the leaves, but Lily had spotted it.

"What's that?" Lily woofed curiously to herself. Even though she knew she ought to get home right away, she couldn't resist having a little look. "I'd better be careful though," she yapped. "It might be dangerous."

So she dropped down onto her tummy, and crawled towards the furry thing. Gently, she reached out a paw to touch it. Nothing happened. "Grr! Who are you?" she growled. "Are you my friend or not?"

The furry thing still didn't speak or move. Lily wondered if it was another dog. But it didn't smell like one. It didn't smell like a cat either. What could it be?

She moved even closer and sniffed it all over. Then she took a good look at it. "Oh, it's a teddy bear!" Lily woofed, delighted. She knew what teddy bears were because Jack had an old bear, Herbie, sitting on his pillow. This teddy looked even tattier than Herbie, though. He was quite dirty and a bit damp, and had a frayed red ribbon round his neck.

Lily didn't care. She was thrilled. She'd gone to find herself a new friend – and she'd found one!

"Come on," Lily woofed, picking the teddy up gently in her mouth. "I'll look after you from now on!" And the teddy bear seemed to smile at her.

Suddenly Lily remembered that Jack was on his way home. If she didn't hurry, he might notice that she wasn't there and get upset.

She quickly raced down the

garden, carrying the teddy. Now,
where was the hole?

For a moment, Lily couldn't
remember exactly where the hole
was. Her heart beat faster. Then
she spotted it, almost hidden
behind a tall tree. She dashed
over to it.

It was even more of a squeeze
for Lily to get through the hole

with the teddy in her mouth. She pushed and heaved and struggled and panted, until finally the two of them were through. Then Lily pushed her way out from behind the bush.

She was just shaking bits of twigs and leaves from her furry coat when the back door opened. Jack and Sally came out into the garden.

"There she is," Jack called, waving to her. "Hi, Lil!"

"What's Lily got in her mouth?" Sally laughed, staring at the excited puppy. "It's nearly as big as she is."

Lily raced towards them, tail wagging, and laid the teddy down gently on the grass. "This is

my new friend," she barked
proudly. Then she launched
herself at Jack for her usual after-
school cuddles.

"Lily, where did you get *that*?"
Jack fussed Lily for a moment or
two, then he picked the teddy up
and examined it. His mum came
out of the house. "Mum, look
what Lily's found," Jack called.

"Oh dear, it's a bit dirty, isn't
it?" Mrs Harper wrinkled her
nose.

"Don't talk about my new friend
like that!" Lily yapped indignantly.

"Lily must have found it in the
garden," Jack's mum went on.
"Maybe it belonged to the people
who lived in the house before we
moved in."

"The people who lived here before you *did* have a little baby," Sally agreed. "Maybe it was his teddy and they left it behind by accident."

Lily was listening with her head cocked to one side. She'd never thought about to whom the teddy might *really* belong. Maybe someone was looking for him right at this minute . . .

But if they really wanted the teddy, they wouldn't have left him out in the rain and the cold, would they? No, Lily decided, the teddy belonged to her from now on.

"Please, Jack, can I play with my new friend?" she barked, pawing impatiently at Jack's legs.

Jack laughed as he bent down to hand Lily the teddy. "There you go, Lil!"

"Oh, Jack," Mrs Harper said crossly. "It's filthy. If Lily wants to play with it, it'll have to be washed first."

"No way!" Lily growled through her teeth. "My teddy's

not having a horrible old bath."
And she shot off into the house.

"I don't think you'll get the
teddy away from her, Mum!" Jack
laughed as they followed Lily
inside.

He was right. Lily loved her
teddy so much, she just wouldn't
put him down. First, she took her
new friend all over the house. She
showed him her food and water
bowls, then her lead and her toys.
Next, she showed him her
favourite snoozing-spot on the
end of Jack's bed. Last of all, she
took the teddy to the living-room
to meet Mr Harper, who was still
struggling to put up the shelf.

When Jack and Sally went to the
corner shop to buy some milk for

Jack's mum, Lily went too, with the teddy clutched proudly in her mouth. Everyone they passed in the street stopped and smiled when they saw the puppy carrying her teddy bear.

"Lily really loves her teddy, doesn't she?" Sally grinned as they walked back from the shop with Lily trotting alongside them.

"I don't think Mum does," Jack replied. "But it looks like Lily's teddy is here to stay."

Lily wagged her tail happily. Jack and Sally were right. Now she had a friend to play with while Jack was at school. Lily felt like the luckiest puppy in the whole world!

Chapter Four

"Come on, Teddy!" Lily woofed, as she climbed through the dog flap. "Let's go out into the garden before Mrs Harper catches us."

It was the following morning. Lily had slept curled up on Jack's bed all night, like she usually did. But this time she'd had Teddy lying beside her.

And when Mrs Harper had popped her head round the door that morning, she'd gasped in dismay. "Oh, Lily! Get that dirty old thing off Jack's bed *at once*!"

"It's OK, Mum," Jack yawned. "I don't mind."

"Well, I do," Mrs Harper said. "That teddy needs a good wash."

"Don't worry, Teddy," Lily barked determinedly. "I'll save you." She grabbed the teddy in her teeth, and charged out of Jack's bedroom.

Lily clattered down the stairs and into the kitchen. It was Saturday, so when Jack had washed and dressed, and had his breakfast, he would be taking Lily for an extra-long walk. Until then, Lily was determined to keep her new friend out of Mrs Harper's clutches.

"Why do people always want to *wash* everything?" Lily whined crossly, as she laid Teddy carefully on the lawn. "Have you ever had a bath, Teddy? It's horrible. All the shampoo gets in your eyes and up your nose, and makes you sneeze."

It was the beginning of a warm, sunny day. Lily left Teddy lying on the grass sunbathing, while she wandered around the garden. She put her nose to the ground, sniffing all the early-morning smells.

"Aha!" she barked. "That cat

from Number 35 has been in here again. Do you like cats, Teddy? I don't."

Lily didn't want to leave her new friend on his own for too long, and soon bounded back across the lawn to him. "What shall we do now, Teddy?" she barked, jumping playfully around the bear. "Oh, I know – I've got a great idea!"

Lily picked Teddy up and headed down the garden towards the hole that led next door. There was more of next door's garden to explore! And maybe, another new friend to be found, hidden under a bush, like Teddy was.

Lily had plenty of time too. Jack had to get washed and dressed and have his breakfast yet. Then he always watched his favourite cartoon on Saturday mornings before they went out for their walk.

Holding Teddy firmly in her mouth, Lily squeezed through the hole again. She trotted out onto the lawn, just as the squirrel ran down its tree.

"Look. I've got a new friend," Lily barked, forgetting that she had Teddy in her mouth. The bear tumbled out onto the grass. "Oops, sorry, Teddy."

Lily was about to pick Teddy up again when she noticed something very interesting. Because it was a warm and sunny morning, the big glass doors at the back of the house were open.

"Look, Teddy!" Lily woofed delightedly. "Let's go and say hello to that man I saw yesterday. I hope he's got some cake left."

The puppy scooped Teddy up and dashed across the lawn towards the open doors.

Lily was just about to rush up

the steps and hurtle into the house when she heard voices. She stopped and listened curiously.

"Grandad, have you found William yet?"

It was a little girl speaking. Lily's ears pricked up. Who was William?

"No, love, I'm afraid I haven't," a man's voice replied.

Lily wondered if it was the old man she'd seen watching TV the day before.

"But he must be *somewhere*, Grandad." The little girl sounded as if she was about to cry. Lily felt very sorry for her. "I know I left him here last time I came to visit."

"Never mind, Amelia," said her grandad gently. "I'll buy you a lovely new teddy bear next time we go to town. You can even choose one with a red ribbon, just like William."

"I don't *want* a new teddy bear – I want to find poor William," Amelia howled. She burst into tears.

Lily's ears went down and her tail stopped wagging. She put her teddy on the steps and stared sadly at him. "Are *you* William?" she whimpered softly. "Do you belong to Amelia?"

Lily didn't know what to do. She loved her teddy very much. But now she'd found out that he belonged to someone else. How would Lily feel if someone took *her* away from Jack, and wouldn't give her back?

Lily's ears perked up, and her tail began to wag again. There was only one thing to do.

Chapter Five

Lily picked up the smiling teddy
bear and climbed the steps
towards the open doors. She
could see Amelia sitting on her
grandfather's knee, while he
wiped her eyes with a big
handkerchief. They hadn't noticed
the puppy at all.

Lily trotted into the house and laid the teddy bear down on the carpet. "Hello," she woofed. "Don't cry, Amelia – look, I found William for you."

Both Amelia and her grandfather jumped when they heard Lily. They turned round, and looked amazed when they saw a puppy sitting there, next to Amelia's teddy.

"It's William!" Amelia gasped, jumping off her grandad's lap.

"And who are *you*?" the old man asked, staring hard at Lily.

"I'm Lily," Lily whimpered. She hoped Amelia and her grandad wouldn't think that she'd *stolen* William. "I really love Teddy – I mean, William – but he's not mine, so I'm giving him back."

Amelia had grabbed William, and was hugging him tightly. "This puppy found William, Grandad!" she said, her eyes shining. She knelt down and put her arm round Lily. "Isn't she clever?"

"Very clever indeed," her grandfather agreed. Lily's stumpy little tail began to wag again. "I wonder where she found him?"

"William's a bit dirty," Amelia said, examining her teddy closely. "Maybe he was in the garden."

"He was!" Lily woofed. "I found him under a bush."

"And where have *you* come from?" The old man bent down stiffly and looked at the identity tag on the puppy's collar. "Look, Amelia, her name's Lily. There's a phone number here too. Maybe we ought to call in case she's lost."

"No, I'm not," Lily barked. "I *never* get lost! Well . . . maybe once or twice . . ."

"Oh, Grandad, *please* can we give Lily a treat for finding William?" Amelia begged, her arm still round Lily's neck. "Before you ring her owner?"

"A treat!" Lily barked, delighted. She gave Amelia a big wet kiss on her cheek. "Yes, please!"

Amelia and her grandad took Lily into the kitchen, and gave her a bowl of cold chicken. Lily wolfed it down, and then followed it with a very small piece of fruitcake she found on the kitchen floor.

While she was eating, Amelia's grandad picked up the phone and rang the number on Lily's collar. "It's engaged," he said, putting the phone down. "Never mind, I'll try again soon."

"Grandad, can I go into the garden and play with Lily?" Amelia asked. She was still clutching William tightly.

Her grandad nodded. "But maybe you ought to give William to me so that I can wash him," he said with a frown. "He'll be dry by the time your mum comes to collect you."

"Oh no, Grandad," Amelia said quickly. "William's fine!" And she dashed off into the garden with Lily at her heels.

"Why do grown-ups always want to *wash* everything, Lily?" Amelia sighed as they ran out onto the lawn.

"I don't know. I don't understand it either," Lily woofed. She was still feeling a bit sorry that she'd had to give Teddy back, but Amelia looked so happy that Lily knew she'd done the right thing. "Come on, let's chase each other up and down the lawn really fast."

Meanwhile, over at the Harpers' house, Jack had finished his breakfast and watched his favourite cartoon. Now he was ready to take Lily for her walk. He had a quick look round his house, but he couldn't find the puppy anywhere.

He went to ask his mum and dad if they'd seen Lily, but

Mr Harper had popped out to buy a newspaper, and Mrs Harper was on the phone to Jack's gran.

"Lily must be in the garden," Jack said to himself, heading for the back door.

Although there was no sign of Lily when he went outside, Jack didn't feel too worried. There were plenty of places in the garden for a small puppy to hide. "Lily!" he called. "Time for your walk!"

He waited. The word *walk* was usually enough to bring Lily running from wherever she was. But this time she didn't appear.

"Lily?" Jack tried again. But still nothing. No brown-and-white bundle rushing towards him, panting and wagging her tail.

Jack began to feel worried. He knew that his mum and dad had made sure that there was no way for the puppy to get out of the garden and wander off. So where on earth could she be? *Surely* she couldn't have got out of the garden, after all?

His heart pounding with fear, Jack cupped his hands to his mouth. "LILY!" he yelled as loudly as he could.

Was he imagining it, or was that a bark he'd heard? Jack listened hard. There it was again, and it seemed to be coming from the bottom of the garden.

Jack raced down the lawn, expecting to see Lily come

dashing out of the thick under-growth towards him. There was still no sign of the puppy, but the barking was getting louder.

Jack pushed his way between the large bushes that stood in front of the fence. "Lily, is that you?" he shouted.

There was another bark, and then a small voice said, "Hello?"

Jack jumped. "Hello," he called. "Who are *you*?"

"I'm Amelia," the girl called back. "Is this your puppy? Her name's Lily."

"Lily's there with *you*?" Jack said, amazed. "In your garden?"

"It's not my garden, it's my grandad's," Amelia explained.

"But how did Lily get in there?"

Jack asked, puzzled.

"I think there's a hole in the fence," Amelia called back. "Lily came in and found my teddy William. I lost him last week."

"So that was *your* teddy!" Jack exclaimed.

"Yes, and Lily gave him back to me," Amelia went on. "She's a really clever puppy."

"I know," Jack said proudly. Just then, there was a rustling in the bushes in front of him.

A moment later, Lily appeared with bits of leaves and twigs stuck all over her. She jumped happily into Jack's arms.

"Lily!" Jack cried, giving her a big hug. "I thought you were lost again!"

"Of *course* I wasn't lost," Lily woofed, licking Jack's nose. "I was just taking William back to his proper owner, that's all!"

Chapter Six

Jack rushed back into the house with Lily to explain what had happened to his mum.

Mrs Harper was just saying goodbye to Jack's gran. But before Jack could say anything, the phone rang again.

It was Mr Roberts. Amelia had

rushed in to explain everything to her grandad too. Mr Roberts invited Lily, Jack and Mrs Harper to pop in and say hello. Lily was delighted.

"Hello, do come in." Amelia's grandfather opened the front door wide, beaming at Mrs Harper, Jack and Lily. "I'm Gerry Roberts, and this is my granddaughter Amelia. Hello again, Lily!"

"Hi!" Lily barked. She rushed over to Amelia, who had William in her arms.

Amelia bent down and gave Lily a cuddle, and Lily gave William a friendly lick.

"Pleased to meet you," said Mrs Harper, shaking hands with

Mr Roberts. "We're so glad that Amelia's got her teddy back."

"Thanks to Lily," Amelia added gratefully, and Lily gave her a wet kiss on the nose.

"Come and have some tea," Amelia's grandad said, leading the way into the living-room.

Lily's tail began to wag like crazy when she saw plates of cakes and biscuits laid out on the table.

"I hope you weren't too worried when you saw that Lily was missing, Jack," said Mr Roberts.

"I was a *bit* worried," Jack admitted with a grin. "You see, Lily's got lost before."

"But I always come back!" Lily yapped, eyeing a plate of

chocolate biscuits.

"Well, we're very grateful to Lily," Mr Roberts went on. "We've been looking for William all week. Amelia was very upset. She's got lots of other teddies, but William's her favourite."

"Grandad." Amelia pulled at her grandad's sleeve. "Can I give Lily her present now?"

"Present?" Lily's ears perked up when she heard that. She *loved* presents. "What is it?" she barked.

Mr Roberts nodded, and Amelia dashed out of the room.

When she came back a moment or two later, she had a small blue teddy in her arms. "This is for you, Lily," she said, holding it out. "His name's Thomas."

Lily could hardly believe her eyes. She went over and sniffed the teddy, then gave him a friendly lick. "A teddy of my own!" she woofed, thrilled to bits.

She gently took Thomas from Amelia's hand, and showed him proudly to Jack.

"Maybe Amelia and William can come round and play with Thomas and Lily sometimes," Jack suggested. He laughed as Lily tugged Thomas out of his hand, and held on to him firmly.

"Well, I often look after Amelia while her mother's at work," Mr Roberts explained. "So maybe Amelia could pop over to see Lily on the days she's not at her nursery school?"

"I think Lily would really love that," Jack agreed.

Lily couldn't say anything, of course, because she was holding Thomas in her mouth, so she just wagged her tail as hard as she could. Now she had *four* new friends: William, Amelia, Mr Roberts – and Thomas!

Lily the Lost Puppy

Will she find her way home?

Lily's family is moving house. Jack, Lily's owner, tells her all about their new home.

Then something terrible happens. Lily's family leave her behind, by mistake. Will Lily ever see Jack again?

Lily at the Beach

She's lost again!

Sandcastles, sea and shells! Lily's so excited: she's off to the beach with Jack.

But Lily's a pup who likes to explore – and she gets into all sorts of trouble!

Collect all of JENNY DALE'S PUPPY TALES™!

JENNY DALE'S PUPPY TALES™

Gus the Greedy Puppy	0 330 37359 5	£3.99
Lily the Lost Puppy	0 330 37360 9	£3.99
Spot the Sporty Puppy	0 330 37361 7	£3.99
Lenny the Lazy Puppy	0 330 37362 5	£3.99
Max the Mucky Puppy	0 330 37363 3	£2.99
Tilly the Tidy Puppy	0 330 37366 8	£3.99
Spike the Special Puppy	0 330 48099 5	£3.99
Hattie the Homeless Puppy	0 330 48107 X	£3.99
Fergus the Friendly Puppy	0 330 48105 3	£2.99
Lily at the Beach	0 330 48427 3	£2.99
Lily Finds a Friend	0 330 48426 5	£3.99